"Silence, please. . . ."

CINDERLILY

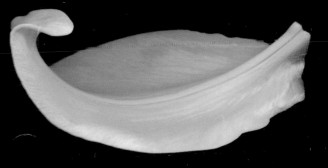

CANDLEWICK PRESS

PRESENTS

Cinderlily

A FLORAL FAIRY TALE

in Three Acts

Directed, designed, and choreographed by

DAVID ELLWAND

Libretto by

CHRISTINE TAGG

CANDLEWICK PRESS

CAMBRIDGE, MASSACHUSETTS

ACT I
The Sultan's Autumn Ball

A FORMAL INVITATION
comes to flowers one AND all:

Please gather
at the Palace for the

ROYAL

AUTUMN BALL.

Tonight the Sultan

will choose his bride—

the loveliest bloom

of all.

One bedraggled flower hears

the news gives a sigh.

Her name is CINDERLILY,

and she's beautiful but shy.

Forlorn and sad, she smoothes her petals—

she's trying not to cry.

Then she hears her sisters calling,
"You must HELP US look our best.
Then surely, at the Sultan's Ball,
we'll STAND OUT from the rest."

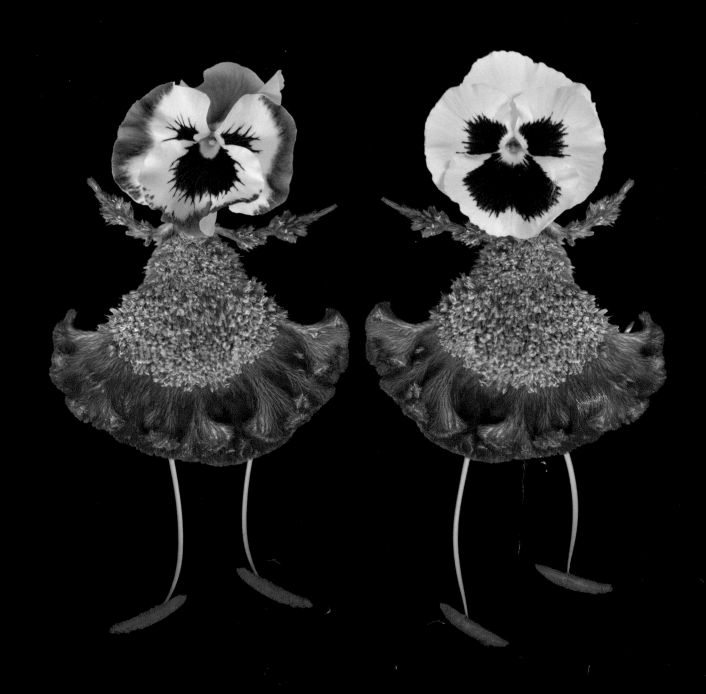

"And as for you, there, Cinderlily,

you simply cannot come.

You'll STAY right here and clean the house

while we are having fun."

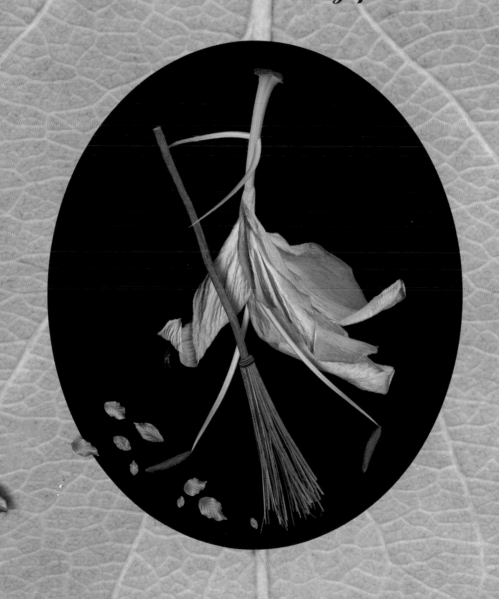

Poor Cinderlily, all alone,

SHE WILL NOT

HAVE A CHANCE.

She'll rub and scrub and dust and sweep

while her mean old sisters dance.

So Cinderlily DAYDREAMS

as she floats around the room.

Twirling lightly round *and* round,

SHE DANCES WITH

HER BROOM.

ACT II
A Fairy Visit

Suddenly a light appears—

a fairy hovers near.

"CINDERLILY, don't despair," she cries,

"now that I am here.

My magic will TRANSFORM you—

with the Sultan you shall dance.

But mind, be back by MIDNIGHT,

or that's the END of the romance."

And so the fairy casts a spell,

and to Cinderlily's SURPRISE . . .

A splendid GOLDEN coach appears,

with six bright butterflies.

When Cinderlily looks again,

her wishes have come true—

her torn and faded petuls

are BLOOMING all ANEW.

At the ball, the handsome SULTAN

greets his eager garden guests.

It's clear from all their gestures

that each HOPES to be the best—

a row of nervous flowers

all keen to pass the test.

To only one he'll give his heart,

to just one bloom his LOVE confess.

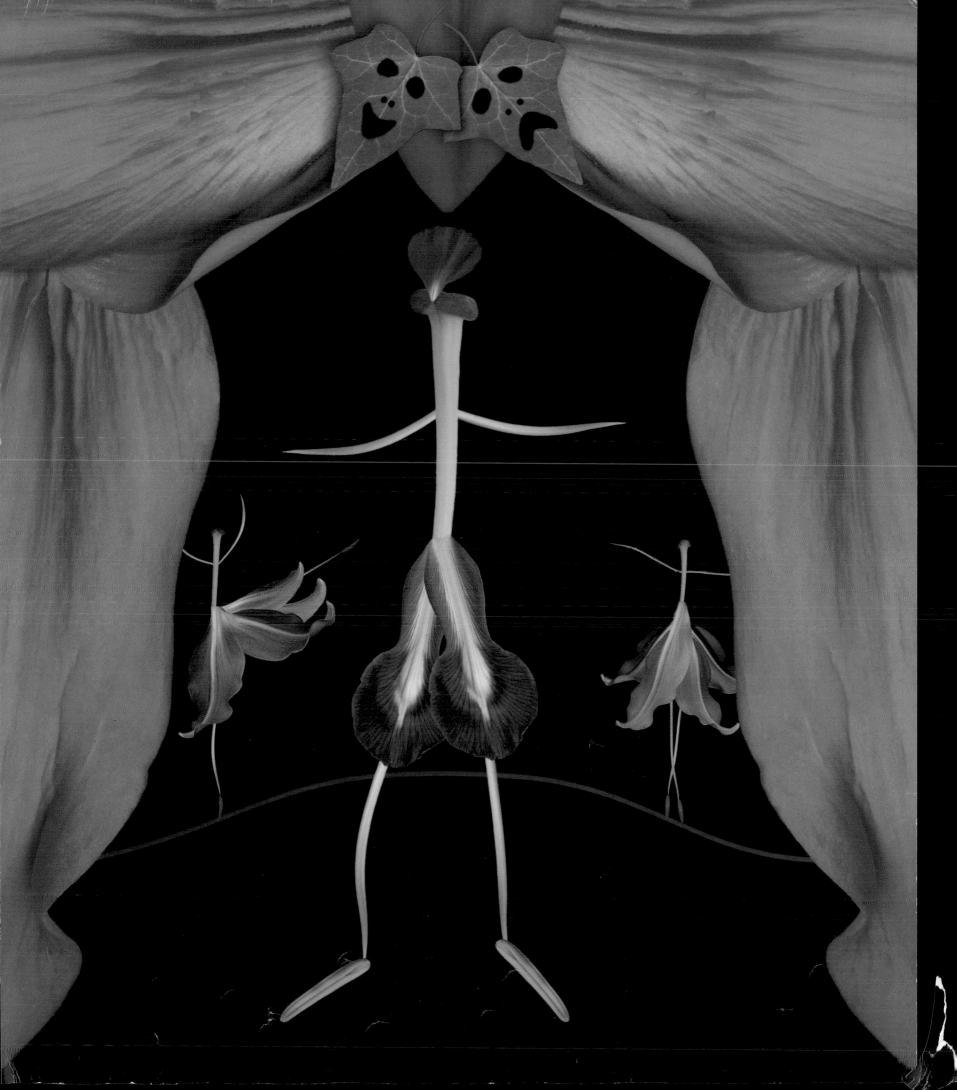

The band strikes up, the music starts,

A WALTZ BEGINS THE BALL.

And as the flowers join the dance,

the Sultan scans the hall.

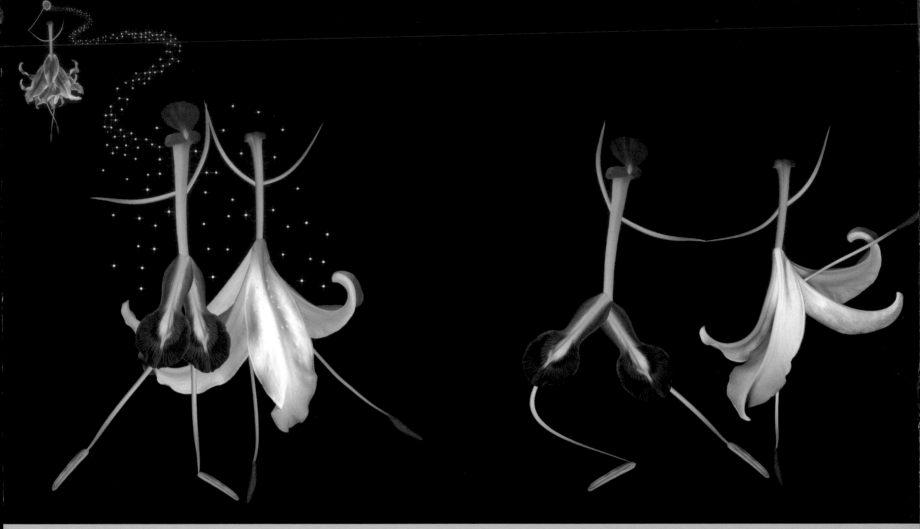

Fluttering near, THE FAIRY knows

the very flower he must meet.

She casts a spell to show him

Cinderlily, SHY AND SWEET.

And when he sees HER LOVELINESS,

HIS HEART near skips a beat.

For hours beneath the velvet sky

THEY DANCE without a care,

until the clock chimes midnight. . . .

Then she's no longer there! Just a SINGLE

lily **PETAL** *and her fragrance in the air.*

ACT III
The Handsome Couple

So the Palace proclaims a search

of gardens FAR AND WIDE.

The petal on a cushion rests,

the Sultan by its side.

"WHOMSO'ER

THIS PETAL FITS

shall be the Royal Bride."

Day by day THE FLOWERS come

to heed the royal call.

The missing petal is gently tried

IN VAIN by one all...

until the Sultan sees, as he

enters one small room,

the faded, UNFORGETTABLE charm

of a once familiar bloom.

"WILL YOU

BE MY BRIDE?" he asks.

"I would gladly be your groom."

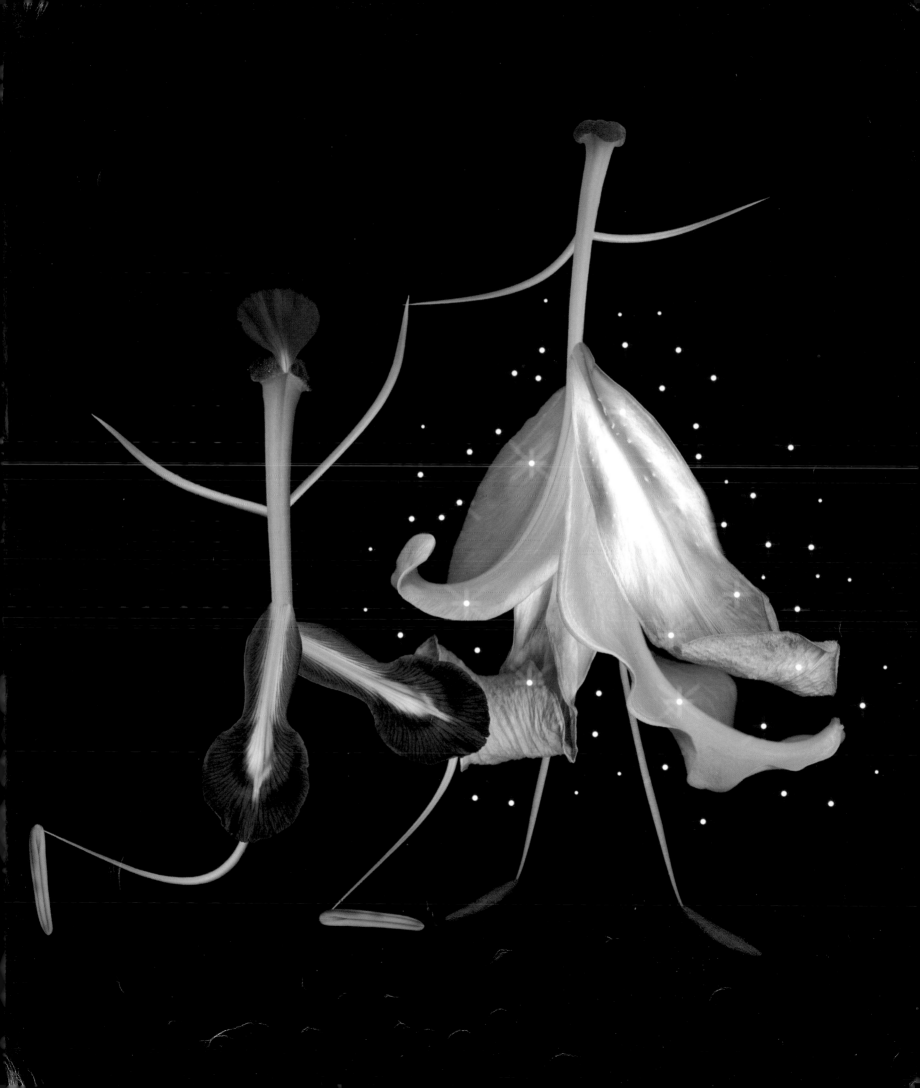

And with dancing petals rising,

a daffodil FANFARE

sounds for the handsome couple

and for fairies everywhere . . .

to CELEBRATE

the MARRIAGE

of such a happy pair.

CANDLEWICK PRESS

HAS BEEN PROUD TO PRESENT

CINDERLILY

A Floral Fairy Tale in Three Acts, adapted from an original story by Charles Perrault

Directed, designed, & choreographed by

DAVID ELLWAND

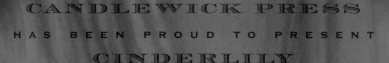 Principal cast:

Lilium Oriental as CINDERLILY

Iris Xiphium as THE SULTAN

Lilium Stargazer as THE FAIRY GODMOTHER

Libretto by CHRISTINE TAGG

Stage management by A.J. WOOD & MIKE JOLLEY

Library of Congress Cataloging-in-Publication Data is available.

Library of Congress Catalog Card Number 2003051598

ISBN 0-7636-2328-8

2 4 6 8 10 9 7 5 3 1

Printed in Hong Kong

This book was typeset in Coronet & Chevalier.

The players in this story were created with
a little ELLWAND magic in Adobe Photoshop.

CANDLEWICK PRESS

2067 MASSACHUSETTS AVENUE

CAMBRIDGE, MASSACHUSETTS 02140

visit us at www.candlewick.com

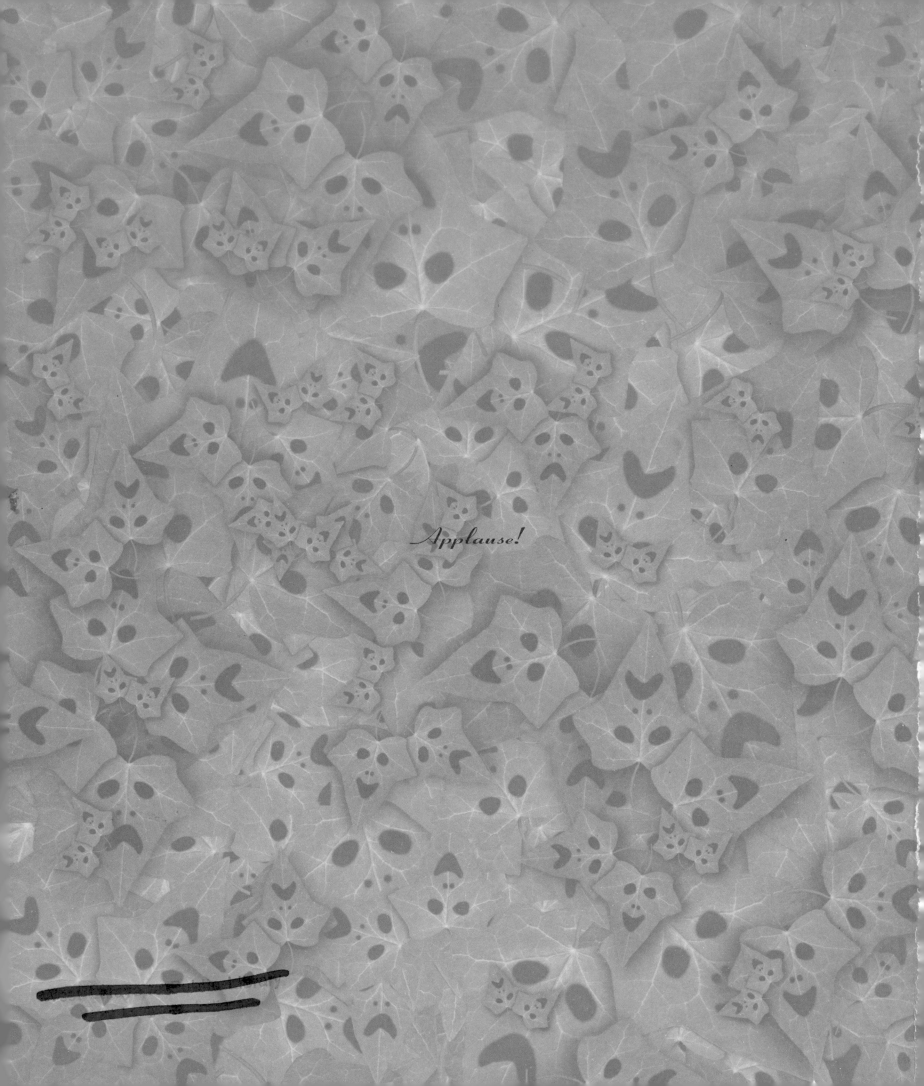

Applause!